Basil Edwards

Songs of a Parish Priest

Third Edition

Basil Edwards

Songs of a Parish Priest
Third Edition

ISBN/EAN: 9783744770309

Printed in Europe, USA, Canada, Australia, Japan

Cover: Foto ©Andreas Hilbeck / pixelio.de

More available books at **www.hansebooks.com**

Songs of a

Parish Priest.

BY

REV. BASIL EDWARDS, M.A.,

LATE OF GONVILLE AND CAIUS COLLEGE, CAMBRIDGE;
RECTOR OF ASHLEWORTH, GLOUCESTER.

AUTHOR OF "JINIFRIED: A LEGEND OF NORTH DEVON."

THIRD EDITION.

GEORGE ALLEN,
LONDON AND ORPINGTON
1892.

PREFACE TO THE THIRD EDITION.

IN the preface to the First Edition of this book the writer expressed his conviction that in every parish and every country village there are, besides the living voice of the Church, numberless silent witnesses which appeal to her sons' and daughters' hearts, and that all the associations, even of the material things which form part of and surround the "houses of God in the land," are intensely sacred and full of teaching; and it was his earnest wish to be enabled, in these hurrying days, to call attention to the ancient and godly doctrine which is thus expressed and handed down from age to age.

The very kind reception given to two previous editions of this little book encourages him to hope that the effort thus made, which has been to him, as a Parish Priest, a daily solace and labour of love, has not been without its uses in awakening a deeper reverence for, and a tenderer appreciation of, the blessings of our common heritage.

PREFACE TO THE SECOND EDITION.

THAT beautiful, but to many little-known, prayer
called the " Bidding Prayer," invites our suffrages
for Christ's Holy Catholic Church, and especially for
that pure and Apostolic branch of it established in
these realms. It has seemed to the writer of this little
book, that in every parish and every country village
there are, besides the living voice of the Church, numberless silent witnesses which appeal to her sons' and
daughters' hearts; and that all the associations, even
of the material things which form part of and surround
the " houses of God in the land," are intensely sacred,
and are full of teaching.

The quiet of a country charge has enabled the writer
to endeavour to link together many of the objects most
prominently connected with sacred thought in a rural
parish, and to present the results to the reader in
somewhat of a sequence, leading step by step from
the Lych Gate to the Altar. If this endeavour serves
at all to deepen the love of sacred things in the hearts
of any of the sons and daughters of the Church, he
will be more than repaid.

PREFACE.

It only remains for him to acknowledge most grate-
fully the kind reception which the First Edition has met
with, both from the Press and the Public, and to hope
that the present issue, in which a few additional poems
have been inserted, may be as fortunate.

CONTENTS.

CONTENTS.

PART II.

PART I.

THE VILLAGE CROSS.

" Having made peace through the blood of His cross."—Col. i. 20.

IN the centre of the village,
　Where the well-worn roadways meet,
And the shadows from the sunset
　Fall slanting o'er the street,
Among the passing people,
　With their ceaseless ebb and flow,
Still rise the ancient stones which bore
　The cross in years ago.

The steps are cut in sevens,
　They are smooth and worn with age,
The relics of a far-off time
　Writ on an elder page.
And here in careless gladness
　The village children play,
Where their forefathers' fathers
　Were wont to kneel and pray.

Here in the westering sunlight,
　Beneath the sacred rood,
In days now long departed,
　The wandering friar has stood,
With arms and voice uplifted,
　To tell of Mary's Son,
Through whose dear cross and passion
　The whole wide world was won.

I

THE VILLAGE CROSS.

The burgher from the city,
  The franklin from the grange,
The palmer back from travel
  In countries far and strange,
With village hinds would gather,
  While tears would sometimes rise,
And gentle looks come softly
  To unaccustomed eyes.

Here, when the waves of battle
  Had broken all in blood,
The flying and the dying
  Would cling around the rood;
The bitter sword of vengeance
  Would turn its edge aside,
Aud brother bend with brother
  Before the "Crucified."

Like some high tower at midnight,
  From which there streams the ray
That cheers and guides the toilers
  'Oer ocean's storm-tossed way;
So, 'midst the lurid darkness
  Of those red feudal skies,
The one great Church was pointing
  The path to Paradise.

And still these stones are standing
  In witness of the past,
With mute appeal to heaven
  Though skies be overcast.
They tell our children's children,
  'Mid earthly gain or loss,
How their forefathers' fathers
  Built up the village cross.

THE VILLAGE SCHOOL.

My little children of whom I travail again in birth until Christ
be formed in you."—*Col.* iv. 19.

WHEN the clock is striking twelve,
　　Before the last note dies,
How eager are the children,
　　With happy, laughing eyes!

And clatter go their footsteps
　　Adown the village street;
Ah! well if in the years to come
　　Life might be found as sweet!

And chatter go their voices,
　　The tones arise and fall—
The rich, full melody of life
　　Is rippling through them all.

Oh, happy burst of laughter,
　　Amid the leafy lanes!
Oh, ringing mirth that eddies round
　　The latticed window-panes!

Oh, clear unsullied gladness!
　　Oh, eyes so innocent!
Ye surely have not dreamed as yet
　　What sin and sorrow meant.

THE VILLAGE SCHOOL.

The fresh, fair sunlight glances
  On each unruffled brow;
O that the stress and strain of life
  Might leave you pure as now!

THE LYCH-GATE.

"This is the gate of heaven."—*Gen.* xviii. 17.

A T the entrance of the Churchyard,
     Where the graves are green and fair,
The old lych gateway standeth
     Above the low mounds there.
A good old oaken gateway,
     Where the priest receives the dead,
Where first the mourners' footsteps
     Pause in their solemn tread.

On one side lies the trampling
     And the noise of the village street,
But within is the holy quiet
     Of a hushed and calm retreat,
Where the very air is clearer,
     And the deep, deep sky more blue,
For the doors of heaven seem nearer,
     As if God were coming through.

Beneath that gabled archway,
     While bells ring soft and clear,
The happy congregations
     Have passed for many a year.
Yet sometimes there in silence
     The eyes of love run o'er,
As some are borne beneath it
     Who come back nevermore.

THE LYCH-GATE.

Yet hence, in youthful gladness,
　The bridegroom leads the bride,
The while the village children
　Gaze on them sunny-eyed.
And words of kindliest greeting
　Full many a time are said,
As friend with friend is meeting
　Beneath the Lych-gate's shade.

The path that winds beneath it
　Is bordered with the sod,
And echoed once with footsteps
　That rest them now with God.
Age after age is travelling
　Along that sacred way,
And where we tread, our fathers
　Were passing yesterday.

And thus that old lych gateway
　Is witness day by day,
When we pass into the churchyard
　To muse awhile and pray,
That in God's gracious keeping
　We too may close our eyes,
And pass beyond its portals
　To sunny Paradise.

THE SATURDAY OF FLOWERS.

"Dydd Sadwrn y Blodan."

I LOVE that old Welsh custom,
  "The Saturday of Flowers,"
Which renders to the hallowed dead
  A few regretful hours.
Before the bells of Easter
  Are throbbing on the air,
Our steps are drawn to holy ground,
  And those who slumber there.

'Twas in Saint Joseph's garden
  They laid Our Lord to rest,
And meetly 'neath the stainless flowers
  His people slumber best.
With God's free winds around them,
  And the soft blue skies above,
While our tender thoughts surround them,
  E'en in their graves, with love.

Each mound is like a garden:
  In clusters here and there,
The simple-hearted country folk
  Their treasured offerings bear.
They have wreaths of pure, pale primrose,
  The emblem meet of rest,
And crosses of Lent lilies
  To lie upon the breast.

They pass in silence, softly,
  Among the quiet dead,
The village children, sunny-eyed,
  With gentle, reverent tread.
And the father trims the hillock,
  While the mother, near the spot,
Is bending o'er the bright fresh tufts
  Of blue "forget-me-not."

There are miners from the "Forest,"
  Stained with the rich red ore,
And fisher-folk from far away
  Beside the Severn shore.
The "fathers of the hamlet"
  Lie 'neath the sacred sod.
They dress the graves, and pause awhile,
  To think of them—and God.

The parish priest among them
  In quiet converse walks,
And, mingling with the changing groups,
  In kindly wise he talks.
His words are to the living,
  Then of the dead, anon,—
Full well of those who slumber there
  He mindeth many a one.

Then, as the soft spring sunset
  Fades on the time-worn towers,
The hues of evening gather round
  The Saturday of Flowers,
All in God's gracious keeping
  We leave the dead to rest,
With the crosses of Lent lilies
  That lie upon the breast.

THE CLOCK.

" Be the day never so long
It ringeth at last to evensong."

THE dial on the good grey tower
Meteth Time's fleeting measure;
The halves, the quarters, and the hour,
Or bring they pain or pleasure.

The gilded hands before the face,
In gladness or affliction,
Like sainted fingers fraught with grace,
Uplift their benediction.

To some its flying moments flit,
Touched with a tinge of glory,
To others as they muse on it
Life shows a sombre story.

Of all the faces far and near,
While Time swings onward slowly;
The features, be they loved or dear,
Yet change in part or wholly.

But yet that well-known face ere now,
Unlined by care or sadness,
Has looked upon the old man's brow,
And on his infant gladness.

Like One whose ever-watchful eye
  "Nor slumbereth nor sleepeth,"
This old-world dial placed on high
  Its solemn vigil keepeth.

The notes are born in eddying sighs,
  When the red sun is setting,
And witness as the daylight dies,
  In spite of our forgetting.

And some day, when those silver chimes
  On other ears are falling,
And we and all our earthly times
  Are passed beyond recalling,

Then in the clearer light that streams
  Where nought of Time can sever,
May we arise from mists and dreams
  And enter life for ever!

THE VANE.

"The sign of the Son of Man, in Heaven."—*St. Matt.* xxiv. 30.

O SLENDER cross that soarest high
  Towards the thunderous skies,
The while the rolling clouds go by,
In which the lightning lies;
  The tempest rocks thee, far-off rood,
Thou bravest all the winds of God.

From sunlit East the breeze may blow,
  From South or icy North,
Or sweep across the Western seas,
  With wild tempestuous wrath.
But yet, whate'er the wind that blows,
The cross nor change nor danger knows.

O blessèd sign, beheld afar,
  Whene'er the day grows old,
Athwart yon clear horizon bar
  A living gleam of gold;
In witness, as the daylight dies,
That yonder there are fadeless skies.

Thy shadow falls on holy ground,
  Across each rounded grave,
While far beneath the gilded vane
  The giant elm trees wave,
But soaring still through shine or mist,
The village spire looks up to Christ.

Earth's mists lie brooding o'er the ground,
  But as they rise they fade;
The eye of faith can aye discern
  The cross above the shade,
As though to teach us even here
The calm of that high atmosphere.

Thus reaching through the clouds of earth,
  As time is hurrying by,
Christ's Holy Church uplifts her face
  To far eternity;
And though the mists may lie below,
God's awful light is on her brow.

Amid the tumult and the storm
  Of worldly gain or loss,
Although the tempests rage and swell,
  She lifts His steadfast cross,
Until shall dawn that longed-for day
  When all the shadows flee away.

THE BELLS.

"Praise Him upon the loud cymbals."—*Psalm* cl. 5.

O HOLY Bells! O happy Bells!
   How clear your music floats,
As though the tones that wander by
   Had caught some angel notes!

In sunny country far away,
   Or by the salt sea foam,
Your notes are notes of Paradise,
   O hallowed bells of home!

I see once more the good grey tower
   Stand stately 'mid the trees,
And hear for one short sacred hour
   The chimes upon the breeze.

The joy bells on a Christmas morn;
   The peal on Easter Day;
The silver voice that, morn by morn,
   Calls "two or three" to pray.

The notes that throb upon the air,
   With echoes far and wide,
As down the churchyard green and fair
   The bridegroom leads the bride.

Or when away amid the hills
  Rings out the plaintive knell ;
As through each rugged bosom thrills
  Thy note, O passing bell !

The labourer stays his sunburnt hand
  To hear the great bell toll ;
A neighbour nears the silent land,—
  " God speed the passing soul."

And through the hamlet far away,
  With measured beat and dread,
The knell from yonder steeple grey
  Goes sounding for the dead.

And some day, when those changing chimes
  Are throbbing through the air,
And fill men's ears in aftertimes,
  Though we shall not be there,

All in a country far away,
  Beyond the salt sea foam,
O that we hear in Paradise
  The blessèd notes of Home !

THE VESTRY.

'There they shall lay their garments wherein they minister, for
they are holy."—*Ezek.* xlii. 14.

A PEACEFUL chamber, hushed and calm,
　　Where tempered light serenely falls,
And sound floats softly like a psalm
That dies at eve in holy walls.

A presence fills the shadowy room,
A fragrance breathes upon the air,
As though there lingered in the gloom
The incense of a good man's prayer.

There many a bride, with winsome grace,
In which a guileless heart bore sway,
Has looked upon her true love's face
And signed her maiden name away.

And here are numbered lists which show
How, though the world is waxing old,
The cross still gleams on childhood's brow,
And lambs are gathered to the fold.

While yonder clasps enclose the leaves
Which tell how surely, day by day,
The tireless reaper binds the sheaves
And bears the wheat and tares away.

And here the white-robed choristers
Raise reverent voices sweet and low;
Till, as the deep-toned organ stirs,
They wend forth slowly two and two.

Then, after "benediction" falls,
A moment's space they all draw nigh,
And pray within these peaceful walls,
Before they lay those white robes by.

And thus this hallowed chamber seems
A portal to Our Father's home;
To which at length, beyond our dreams,
The footsteps of His children come,—

Where saints shall wear the robes of white
And never lay them more aside,
But gladdened by eternal light
The pure in heart are satisfied.

THE PORCH.

"This is none other but the house of God."—*Gen.* xxviii. 17.

WHEN once within the harbour,
  Its sure protection gained,
The storm-bound vessels anchor,
  Though every cord be strained.
Although the foam is flying
  Beyond the surf-beat "bar,"
The mariners are lying
  Where peace and safety are.

And thus those time-worn portals,
  That rise so calm and grey,
Hold out to wistful mortals
  Their shelter day by day.
Without may be the burden
  Of a life of pain and care,
But within the calm and quiet
  Of Our Father's House of Prayer.

The happy village children
  Pass in with softened tread,
The maiden and the matron,
  The hoary good grey head.
Some think to enter often
  For years and years to come,
And some, a few more footsteps
  They know will bring them home.

So through the vaulted archway
 That leads to yonder door
Men pass alike as brothers,
 And shall do evermore.
All in the same High Presence,
 Within the same grey walls,
Kneel high-born men and lowly,
 As Benediction falls.

And some day, when our footsteps
 No longer tread this way,
Or seek those sacred portals
 Through which they pass to-day,—
When other knees are bending,
 And other voices rise,
Oh to have part unending
 Of praise in Paradise!

THE FONT.

"The washing of regeneration."—*Titus* iii. v.

O ANCIENT stone where, one by one,
   Each village mother brings her child,
To bathe beneath the cleansing flood,
From whence she bears it undefiled!

The generations come and go,
And heads of down are heads of grey;
While those who here were prayed for, come
Themselves in turn to kneel and pray.

Wave after wave of mortal life
Breaks round thee, O thou timeworn stone;
Wave after wave of strain and strife,
But still the tide is rolling on.

The pleading priest, the white-robed choir,
The locks with sacred waters wet,
The infant chrisom-vestured forms,
The brows whereon the cross is set.

And still the ancient grace prevails,
Although the world is waxing old,
" By water and the word," and thus
The lambs are gathered to the fold.

THE FALD-STOOL.

'Let them say, Spare thy people, O Lord.'—*Joel* ii. 17.

BETWEEN the porch and the altar,
  Where the people kneel and pray,
As you pass towards the chancel,
  The Fald-stool stands alway.
And there that intercession
  Which time the more endears
Rolls on its pleading accents
  Through all the changing years.

The voices of our fathers
  Have swelled that tide of prayer,
That mighty supplication
  Has softened many a care.
And surely still those pleadings
  On yon eternal shore
In waves of intercession
  Keep breaking evermore.

Oh, none so high and stately,
  Oh, none so mean and poor,
But both alike are welcomed
  Within the church's door.
The monarch in his splendour,
  The poor man wandering by,
Alike have place and portion
  In that grand Litany.

As God's blue sky is bending
  Upon the far-off hills,
Or as the dew descending
  That feeds a thousand rills,
Or like the mighty ocean
  That washes every shore,
So here each heart's emotion
  Finds echo evermore.

O waves of intercession,
  O suffrages that rise
In lofty, long procession
  Towards eternal skies,
How tender are the memories
  Your holy voices bear,
In all the measured cadence
  Of this so matchless prayer!

Soft as a mother's accents,
  When for her child she pleads,
The voice of our true Mother,
  As thus she intercedes.
And thus her sons and daughters,
  As life is eddying by,
Pour out their hearts in worship
  And bless her Litany.

THE LECTERN.

" All the people were very attentive to hear him."—St. Luke xix. 48.

WITHIN our village chancel,
    Inside the dark oak choir,
Is a spot where the great east window
    Floods all the floor with fire,
Where the gold and crimson glories
    Of its painted lights are thrown,
As the shadows o'er the altar
    Lie floating on the stone.

There stands the wide-wing'd eagle,
    The symbol of Saint John;
Though some who were gathered round it
    Are into silence gone,
Yet it stands with tireless pinions,
    As it bears God's word of grace,
With an onward gaze and upward
    Upon its changeless face.

And, like some silver clarion,
    From where that lectern stands,
Ring daily, softly, clearly,
    The notes of Christ's commands,
The Sower's hand is sowing
    Whene'er he turns those leaves ·
Oh that the last great harvest
    May show the whitening sheaves!

Here no caprice or passion
  Can urge its changeful sway,
God's very words—they only—
  Are set forth day by day.
Oh, wisdom of our fathers,
  To give us daily bread,
As in the Church's order
  Our Master's words are said !

Around that lectern gather,
  While pass the fleeting years,
Eyes that are bright with gladness,
  Some that are soft with tears ;
The light of children's faces,
  Youth, with its open brow,
The earnest gaze of manhood,
  The old man's crown of snow.

So on that spot for ever
  God's message ringeth clear,
Though changing tones and voices
  May bear it to the ear.
And one day, ah ! so surely,
  Although the ages wane,
The bread cast on the waters
  Shall all be found again.

THE PULPIT.

"And Ezra the scribe stood upon a pulpit."—*Neh.* viii. 4.

IT is but a village pulpit,
  It has stood where it stands for years,
And footsteps that now are silent
  Have trodden those oaken stairs;
But at last they have reached a region
  Where the preacher's voice is hushed,
Where stilled is all passionate pleading,
  And the eloquent lips are dust.

It has rung with the soaring echoes
  Of a voice that is far away,
And those panels have thrilled with the music
  Of a tongue that is turned to clay.
But the thoughts which were brave and kindly,
  And the flash of the fearless eye,
Like the love of the Christlike spirit,
  Are things that can hardly die.

It may be some words were homely,
  But they flowed from a true, brave heart,
Which could throb with a brother's gladness,
  Or ache with a sister's smart.
If they knew not the pointless phrases
  Of a school that was Low or High,
Yet they taught of a God who loved us,
  And they branded a lie, a lie.

There's many a toilworn peasant,
  When the work of the week is done,
Who will gaze at this old oak pulpit,
  And sigh for a face that's gone,
For the voice that rang out like silver,
  For the locks like the silver too,
For the eyes which were calm and kindly,
  With the light that was shining through.

It is but a village pulpit,
  It has stood where it stands for years,
But some, as they gaze upon it,
  See dimly through mists of tears,
As they long for the pleading music
  Of a voice that is far away;
For the seed that was sown in weakness
  Lives on in some hearts to-day.

THE ORGAN.

"They rejoice at the sound of the organ."—*Job* xxi. 12.

IN the placid depths of ocean
　　Giant forces are at rest;
All the tumult of the tempest
　　Underlies that peaceful breast.
Storm and whirlwind, crested billow,
　　Wreathen foam, all white and free,
Mighty strength that is resistless,
　　Slumber in a summer sea.

So within these quiet portals,
　　What a storm of music floats,
As the organ's thunder rolleth
　　Upward with exultant notes;
While the great "Amen" goes throbbing
　　Through the arches high and dim,
Till the chords that rise so grandly
　　Wander towards the seraphim!

Onwards, like a tide of glory,
　　Waves of sound go rolling by,
Clinging to the clerestory,
　　Soaring to the songs on high;
Till the soul, awhile transfigured,
　　Seemeth for a moment's space
To have cast aside its raiment,
　　And to touch some far-off place.

Soon this fleeting generation,
  Where we play awhile our part,
Shall have swept into the silence
  That shall hush each restless heart;
But that high triumphant music
  Through these vaulted aisles shall roll,
And each deep " Amen " resounding
  Waken echoes in the soul.

When our barque has reached the haven,
  Other ships shall sail the seas;
When our feeble touch is silent,
  Other fingers sweep the keys;
When the wave has burst in splendour,
  Other billows reach the shore:
Thus the round of laud and worship
  Rolleth onwards evermore.

But within that region saintly,
  Hidden from our eager eyes,
Which we scan in part and faintly,
  Known to us as Paradise,
There are sweeter voices singing
  Than we hear within the choir,
Fuller, richer notes are ringing,
  Grander music, soaring higher.

When the organ's tones no longer
  Fall upon our listening ears,
Or its mighty chords of passion
  Thrill the kneeling worshippers,
May the trembling "vox humana"
  Change into the "voix céleste,"
And the songs that know not sorrow
  Be our loudest—grandest—best !

THE ALTAR.

"We have an altar."—*Heb.* iii. 10.

SIX cities stood in Holy Land:
　　Within their walls dwelt peace,
The fierce avenger stayed his hand,
　　The flying footsteps cease;
Nor sword, nor scath, nor peril waits
The fugitive within those gates.

And so, amidst the storms of life,
　　One place alone is found
Where reverent hearts and feet may press,
　　And find it "Holy Ground";
One spot on earth is free from care,—
Thine altar, Lord, when Thou art there!

It may be but a village shrine,
　　Where two or three may meet
With Him, whose tender love divine
　　Would woo them to His feet;
But yet, what awe and rapture thrill
The faithful few who worship still!

When, rapt in deep adoring awe,
　　The soul to God draws near,
The mists of time are rolled away,
　　The lights of heaven appear;
And e'en on earth, a moment's space,
Our eyes are on "Our Father's" face.

The mystery of mysteries
　Upon that altar lies ;
Bow down, O heart, bow down, O head !
　But, faith, uplift thine eyes :
The very God is at thy side—
Thy gaze is on the Crucified !

And so, amidst our daily cares,
　One harbour lies secure,
Where souls may anchor in the peace
　Of God for evermore,
A shelter where awhile is given
To breathe on earth the air of heaven.

O one tremendous Sacrifice,
　We plead Thee yet again ;
In life and in the days of health,
　In death or mortal pain,
We still would keep Thy sacred tryst,
And meet Thee in Thy Eucharist.

THE CROSS.

"IN HOC SIGNO."

GLIDING through the shadows,
   Goes the cross of Christ,
Through the dreary darkness,
   Through the driving mist.
Lo! the storms are rising;
   Hark! the winds are shrill;
But the cross is moving
   Onwards, onwards still.

Onwards, upwards, homewards
   Through the striving air,
Press the streaming pennons
   Of that standard fair;
Tens and tens of thousands,
   Martyr, child, and maid,
March beneath the shelter
   Of its sacred shade.

Round that waving banner,
   While the war goes on,
Deeds of saintly daring
   Have been wrought and won.
O for feet to follow!
   O for hands to fight!
O for strength to wrestle
   Onwards into light!

Onwards where the battle
   Fierce and fiercer grows,
Where the air is parted
   With a thousand blows,
See the swords are flashing,
   See the spears are wet,
But that lofty banner
   Surgeth onwards yet.

Down the darksome valley
   Streams that sacred sign,
'Midst the gloom and blackness
   How its splendours shine!
Lighting yonder waters,
   Swift and deep and chill,
As its rays are passing
   Onwards, onwards still.

By Thy pangs and passion,
   By Thy pain and loss,
Crucified, we cry Thee,
   Draw us by that cross;
By the wounds of pity,
   By the nail-pierced hand,
Lead Thy pilgrim soldiers
   Into Holy Land.

THE ALTAR LIGHTS.

"The chancels shall remain as they have done in times past."
Rubric.

TWIN lights upon the altar,
   O emblems meet and right,
Ye speak of One whose radiance
   Gives all His people light;
The altar were ungarnished
   Without your sacred ray;
The Church's gold were tarnished
   If He were far away.

Like two clear lamps whose splendour
   Glows softly near and far,
Your rays unite and witness
   The Bright and Morning Star;
They tell of One whose mercy
   Is linked with each behest,—
"My presence shall go with thee,
   And I will give thee rest."

There's light upon the altar,
   And light within the heart
That, like the Holy Mary,
   Pursues the better part.
And, as that sacred Presence
   Breathes like an air divine,
In contrite hearts and humble
   It makes its wondrous shrine.

In many a vast cathedral
  Your rays fall full and fair
And flood the kneeling thousands,
  While God Himself is there ;
Or in some village chancel
  The sacred sign is set,
Within the same high Presence,
  Where " two or three are met.

And so ye deck our altars,
  Though ages come and go,
The Church nor stoops nor falters
  But shines with steadfast glow,—
The guide to yonder city,
  Upon the sinless shore,
Where light of earthly candle
  Is needed nevermore.

THE PATEN.

"The communion of the Body of Christ."—1 *Cor.* x. 16.

O PATEN, smooth with use
  Of service years ago,
A purer ray is thine to-day
  Than earthly splendours show!

No Cæsar's lofty seat,
  Or throne of emperor,
Hath e'er been pressed by such a Guest
  As thou art wont to bear.

For hands that grasp the palm
  Have held thy living bread;
Around thee gleam, as in a dream,
  The shadowy featured dead.

Oh, what an atmosphere
  Of rapture and of prayer,
In awe profound hath dwelt around
  The burden thou dost bear!

The generations pass
  And day succeeds to day;
Though art is long, yet death is strong;
  The river glides away.

But still the Cross retains
Its high unbending faith ;
Though ebb and flow lay kingdoms low,
Yet life o'ercometh death.

The yearning souls of men
Are fed with heavenly food ;
'Mid .pain and strife, they taste of life,
Christ's Body and His Blood.

THE CHALICE.

"The communion of the Blood of Christ."—1 *Cor.* x. 16.

I LIKE to think this slender rim,
   Which holds that crimson flow,
Was pressed by our forefathers' lips
   Two hundred years ago,—

That while the world goes rolling by,
   In dull or fevered mood,
The one true Church is nurtured on
   Christ's Body and His Blood.

And thus this cup, where tremble still
   Those drops so dearly shed,
Was often held by holy hands,
   Now folded with the dead;

And lips that gently touched this rim
   Of silver worn and bright
Are singing with the seraphim
   In everlasting light.

The wistful, reverent, yearning eyes,
   That fell before the rail,
Have opened since in Paradise,
   And see beyond the veil.

While we are chanting in the choir,
  Those sweeter voices raise
The soaring songs that wander far
  Beyond our mortal praise.

But still those hearts that rest them now
  In that serener air
Beat on in unison with ours,
  That sometimes ache with care.

So well we love this chalice bright,
  Our fathers pressed before;
But oh, to drink the wine of God
  On high for evermore!

THE CHALICE VEIL.

"These Holy mysteries."

WHEN downwards from the Holy Mount
　　The feet of Moses trod,
There glowed upon his radiant brow
　The awful light of God;
And none of all the chosen race
Could gaze into that shining face.

When o'er the outspread mercy seat
　The bright Shekinah shone,
One footstep through the rolling year
　Might enter there alone,
And pass unseen by mortal eye
Beyond that veil of mystery.

Yet faith the same high Presence hails
　Within these courts to-day,
Thy people at Thy altar rails
　(Ah, who so blest as they!)
May kneel and keep Thy sacred tryst,
And Thou art with them, Saviour-Christ.

And though a veil of spotless white
　Doth hide the heavenly food,
And screen from man's too eager sight
　The Body and the Blood,
Yet still where sense and sight must cease
The soul can rest herself in peace,—

In perfect peace that questions not
  Of either how or where,
But dwells in the stupendous truth
  That Thou Thyself art there ;
And in the joy that knowledge brings
Is lost to sense of smaller things.

And some day, in God's perfect time,
  Our last communion made,
That Presence, all revealed, shall shine
With rays that cannot fade,
And lighten that tremendous day
Which rends the veil of life away.

HOLY COMMUNION.

"I Believe . . . in the Communion of Saints.

BEFORE one altar kneeling
   We worshipped side by side,
Thy sacred Presence feeling,
   O Jesu Crucified!
With angels and archangels
   We offered praise and prayer,
But some who knelt beside us
   No more may worship there.

Yet in the high thanksgiving
   We deem they bear their part;
The blessed dead, the living,
   Alike are one in heart;
Although those holy voices
   Have soared to loftier strains,
The one great Church rejoices,
   And fellowship remains.

Then pray we for the living,
   Then plead we for the dead,
(For quick and dead are gathered
   In one, the only Head,)
From "glory unto glory"
   That those may take their way;
For grace that these may follow
   To greet them if they may.

The family hath members
  That dwell 'neath sundered skies,
And some are here as pilgrims,
  And some in Paradise.
For though awhile divided
  The severed hosts may be,
'Tis still the same great army
  On either side the sea.

And so in full communion
  We offer praise and prayers,
They in our hearts remembered,
  As we are borne in theirs.
At one High Altar kneeling,
  We worship side by side;
The same dread Presence feeling,
  O Jesu Crucified!

THE POCKET COMMUNION SERVICE.

"Be ye clean that bear the vessels of the Lord."—*Isa.* lii. 11.

ONLY a silver paten,
  Such as a priest may bear
When he treads in men's darkened chambers
  In the hours of their pain and care.
But the eyes that have watched that circlet,
  Where the heavenly food hath lain,
Have opened at length in gladness,
  And for ever have done with pain.

Only a slender chalice,
  With a worn and a shining rim,
But it may be the lips that pressed it
  Now join in the angels' hymn ;
That the words of that last communion,
  As they faded and died away,
Were the notes of Our Father's welcome
  To a feast that is spread for aye.

Only a sound of weeping,
  And the rush of the blinding tears,
While the touch of an angel's fingers
  Unloosened the ties of years,
As the chamber was full of a Presence
  That the watchers might hardly see,
And the breezes were ruffled a moment
  With the breath of eternity.

Only a silver chalice,
  A paten a priest might bear,
But it may be some souls were strengthened
  By the Presence that lingered there.
As they gleamed on some bedside altar,
  Ah! sceptre and diadem
Were dull to the awful radiance
  Of the splendour that clung to them.

At the end of the toilworn pathway,
  On the shore of eternal things,
Where the shadows of time are shaken
  With the rush of the angels' wings,
There may shine on the wasted features
  A light from a far-off place,
And a nimbus that falls from heaven
  Will gleam for a moment's space.

Some day, when our last communion
  And the story of life are o'er,
When the touch of those sacred vessels
  Can come to our lips no more,
Then the light of that long-loved Presence,
  Here worshipped awhile by faith,
Will guide us beyond the shadows,
  Through the grave and the gate of death.

THE ALMS DISH.

"The Lord remember all thy offerings."—*Psalm* xx. 3.

A WIDOW'S hand in days of old
  Gave more than all beside ;
Her gift more costly far than gold,
  Bestowed with careless pride.
So love that yieldeth all must be
The first free gift we bear to Thee.

Thy treasury is open still,
  And there our gifts may pour :
The contrite heart, the subject will
  Are offerings evermore,
Which even Thine all-searching eyes
May gaze upon and not despise.

Within one broadening stream unite
  The alms of rich and poor,
All equal in Thy holy sight,
  Who press Thy temple floor;
How vain all earthly pride and place,
When God and man are face to face!

The silver and the gold are Thine,
  We give Thee but Thine own,
Whene'er within Thy sacred shrine
  We lay our offerings down ;
Yet pleading, Great High Priest, receive
The lowly gifts Thy children give.

They lie upon Thine altar now,
  The while we kneel in prayer ;
O knit again each broken vow,
  That faith may conquer care ;
Grant grace and peace, that life may be
An offering sacred all to Thee.

A FLOWER SERVICE.

"Thou hast the dew of thy youth."—*Psalm* cx. 3.

THE myrtles and the lilies,
　The roses red and white,
In all their blended sweetness,
　Within these walls unite;
From many a stately mansion,
　From many a poor man's home,
As gifts upon God's altar,
　The buds and flowerets come.

Sweet is the scent of violets,
　Borne on the breath of spring,
But sweeter children's praises,
　That rise with heavenward wing;
And clearer than the dewdrop,
　That trembles on the spray,
The holy eyes of childhood,
　When it kneels down to pray.

And some have brought the lily,
　The Blessed Virgin's flower,
And some the soft moss roses
　From sheltered nook and bower;
While others searched with gladness
　In many a lonely spot,
To bring, as offerings, masses
　Of blue " forget-me-not."

And One, be sure, observeth
   The lightest service done,
The cup of water offered
   To cheer some suffering one;
And He who watched the lilies,
   And notes the wild bird's wing,
It may be, will remember
   The flowers the children bring.

The fast unrolling future,
   Amid its fleeting hours,
Will scatter round their pathway
   Its sunshine or its showers;
And as on yonder altar
   The summer's wreath is laid,
May those who brought them blossom
   Where nothing bright can fade!

There is a radiant garden,
   Though no man yet may see,
In all that far-off country,
   How fair its flowers may be;
Oh that the sunny faces
   Amid these buds to-day
May there be safely gathered,
   For ever and for aye!

MINISTERING SPIRITS.

TO MY ANGEL.

"Are they not all ministering spirits, sent forth to minister them who shall be heirs of salvation "—*Heb.* i. 14.

I CANNOT see thy shining wings,
  Or note thy raiment white,
Or greet thee when the morning brings
  Its flood of golden light.
I may not hear thy glorious voice
  On yon serener air,
But yet I bless thee, angel mine,
  For all thy wistful care.

Thou gazest on "Our Father's" face,
  I may not gaze on thine,
Or meet those sinless eyes, or trace
  Thy features line by line.
Enough for me that far away,
  ·In yonder holy land,
The Lord of angels bids me know,
  My elder brethren stand.

Thine eyes and mine have never met,
  They may not meet for years,
Until mine own are closing fast
  To earthly smiles and tears.

Perchance, in that stupendous hour,
  The veil of flesh may lift,
And show the nimbus round thy brow,
  Like sunlight through a rift.

Thy gentle hands, perchance, ere now,
  Have folded to thy breast
The passing souls that sped their way
  To everlasting rest.
The fair, far land of Paradise
  Glowed softly through the mist,
Till thou hadst laid them gently down
  Before the feet of Christ.

I know not yet how much I owe
  To thy unslumb'ring care,
What foes thy arm has warded off,
  O warrior angel fair;
But ah! the waywardness of years
  Might move thee well to scorn,
But that thy love is wonderful,
  My brother elder born.

The Lord of angels and of men
  In one fair chain of love
Hath bound His lowly brethren here
  With those who serve above.
And thus I hail thee, far away,
  Till faith be changed to sight,
Until I greet thee face to face,
  O guardian angel bright!

SILENT VOICES.

"He being dead yet speaketh."—*Heb.* xi. 4.

A PILE of forgotten sermons,
   Dim with the dust of years,
But yet they once were watered
   With loving thoughts and prayers.
And to think that the voice that uttered
   The truths still written here,
With God's own radiant angels
   Has spoken many a year!

You may say that the views seem narrow,
   But I know that the heart was wide,
And the clear keen truth fell kindly
   From a tongue that never lied;
You may call them, now, old-fashioned,
   But they checked some sins, I know,
And they led some steps towards heaven,
   In the days so long ago.

They are only the earnest pleadings
   Of a faithful parish priest,
Which breathe in these faded writings,
   Dusty and worn and creased.
But Truth is the Truth for ever,
   And though he has passed away,
The words of these faded sermons
   Will start into life some day.

Ears that once heard them lightly,
　Hearts that were cased in pride,
Hands that clasped gain so tightly,
　Feet that have stepped aside:
All at the last must gather,
　Keeping the one great tryst,
Neighbour and friend and father,
　All at the feet of Christ.

Only a pile of sermons,
　Bread on the waters thrown ;
"Vox et præterea nihil,"
　Scattered, and lost, and gone.
But Truth is the Truth for ever,
　And these hidden seeds shall rise
When the sheaves are brought home with
　　shouting
　To the garner of Paradise.

THE RECTORY.

"Here we have no continuing city."—*Heb.* vii. 24.

A GABLED house amid the trees,
　　A porch, an ever-open door;
The peaceful murmur of the bees,
A pathway trodden by the poor.

A garden all the children love,
An orchard, and a brook thereby;
A stone's throw from the ancient walls
God's Acre, where we all must lie.

A home in which to spend by faith
Life's little round of hopes and fears;
A home to which in after days
The children's hearts shall turn for years.

Old rooms where fresh young voices rise,
Stone mullions where gold lichens grow,
And casements which the westering skies
Touch with their own far roseate glow.

The study wainscot, dark with age,
Has something sacred in its gloom;
What hands have turned the sacred page!
What prayers ascended from the room!

And some day, when the windows white
Tell all the hamlet "parson's gone,"
O that within the country bright
The Master's lips may say, "Well done."

AMEN.

THE OLD PATHS.

" Ask for the old paths."—Jer. v. 16.

THE good old Church of England,
　　The ancient Faith and Line,
She draws her strength and virtue
　　From Christ the Heavenly Vine.
This Church, which was our fathers',
　　Is ours,—nor ours alone,
For it shall be our children's
　　When we ourselves are gone.

Her threefold cord abideth,
　　The links lead back to Christ;
She breathes Her Master's message,
　　And all may heed who list.
For still His gracious accents
　　Ring in His servants' ears,
"Lo, I am with you alway
　　Throughout the changing years."

The battle grows around her,
　　The sounds of strife are shrill,
But yet the Cross her banner
　　Goes surging onwards still.
Though error's Babel legions
　　Conspire to lay her low,
Yet *"in hoc signo vinces"*
　　Is shining on her brow.

What though the love of many
   Perchance be waxing cold,
And robber hands would plunder
   Her silver and her gold?
Ten thousand times ten thousand,
   Her own true children rise
To meet the world in conflict,
   With eager, fearless eyes.

O mighty Church of England,
   Through thee our land is blessed,
Thy myriad sons and daughters
   Yet love their mother's breast.
For thee our fathers witnessed
   In blood and fire and flame ;
For thee their children's children
   Would even dare the same.

They kneel before thy altars,
   Their voices rise to God,
They walk within those pathways
   Which sainted feet have trod.
The suffrages of ages
   Breathe on their lips to-day,
When in thy holy places
   Thy children kneel and pray.

They prize thine ancient Order,
   They hold the three great Creeds,
That Litany of ages
   Which still so softly pleads ;
And come what may of trial,
   Of storm or strife or ill,
Christ's ancient Church in England
   Shall be our children's still.

IMMOTA FIDES.*

DEDICATED BY PERMISSION TO THE LATE BISHOP OF SALISBURY.
Music by REV. S. G. EDWARDS, *Abingdon, Berks.*

OUR Mother Church of England   A faith - ful witness bears,

'Midst peace and happy sunshine, Or strife, and storm, and tears

The world may rage around her,   Or Tempest's voice may roar,

But One who stills the tumults Is with her ev-er-more. A-men.

* Leaflets of the above Hymn and Tune can be procured from the
Author. Price, post free, **6d.** per dozen.

Built on the sure foundation
  Of Christ th' eternal Word,
She shows the need of cleansing
  By water and by blood :
Taught by the sacred pages,
  She holds the Orders three,
That those who preach glad tidings
  May serve in just degree.

Within her grand Communion,
  Throughout the ages gone,
The noblest hearts of England
  Have rested, one by one :
Her very dust is sacred,
  Her very stones are dear,
Her hallowed shrines have witnessed
  The prayer, the praise, the tear.

Within her walls, our fathers
  Have often knelt in prayer,
And mothers for their children
  Have softly pleaded there :
Voice after voice grows silent,
  Age after age goes by,
And still our lips are breathing
  The same sweet Liturgy.

The battle cry is sounding,
  Sad schism holds her tryst,
And hell makes fiery onslaughts
  Against the fold of Christ.
But like her glorious Master,
  She scarcely deigns reply,—
And while her foes malign her
  She lifts the cross on high.

There may be foes around her
  Who make an angry stir,
But thousands more would offer
  Their hearts' best blood for her ;
It is not yet extinguished—
  The ardour of our sires,
The faith that trod the scaffold
  And fed the martyr-fires.

Our Mother Church of England,
  O Saviour, keep her pure !
O Holy Spirit, guide her ;
  And lead her evermore !
O Triune God, defend her
  Till earth's long night be past,
And o'er the seething waters
  The daybreak stream at last ! Amen.

BATTLE MUSIC.

"Speak unto the children of Israel, that they go forward."
Exod. xiv. 15.

THE golden gates are parted,
    The awful veil is torn ;
The path is plain to follow
    Which sainted steps have worn.
Now who will bear Christ's armour,
    And with His sword on thigh,
Beneath His shining standard,
    Be bold to do or die ?

The spears are sharp and eager
    That hedge Emmanuel's land ;
The foes are keen and countless
    As grains of ocean sand.
No pathway strewn with roses,
    The track is stern and strait,
But yet it leadeth upwards
    To yonder gleaming gate.

Not one swift rush of battle,
    Not one fierce wrench of pain,
But years and years of fighting
    May mark the long campaign.

The hero hearts beside us
  Fall fighting one by one,
Full weary are the warriors
  Before the march is done.

Not always open conflict,
  But ofttimes secret war,—
The toil, the snare, the ambush,
  The sting, the scorn, the scar.
Hell's fiery darts are hurtling,
  Not only in the light,
But in each darkened chamber,
  Beneath the curtains white.

Hands that are hot with fever,
  Eyes that are wet with tears,
Hearts that are sorely riven
  With pangs and pains and fears,
Feet that are very weary,
  All have their part to play
Before the tides of battle
  Shall roll their waves away.

The serried ranks are frowning,
  Yet some have safely pass'd,
And laid the dinted armour
  Aside in peace at last.
Our elder warrior brethren
  Around the gateway stand,
And grasp the guerdon given
  By yonder nail-pierced Hand.

The festal halls are lighted,
  Our feet may win them too ;
What saints have borne and suffered
  Still saints may dare and do.
The foemen's swords are flashing :
  How keen each angry blow !
But soon the peaceful garlands
  Shall bind the patient brow.

Then lift the drooping standards,
  And fight the fight of God ;
The solemn march we travel
  The victor hosts have trod.
Courage, true hearts ! and onwards,
  Look up, ye tear-dimmed eyes,
And join the shining legions
  That press to Paradise !

AT THE THRESHOLD.

"Behold, I stand at the door and knock."—*Rev.* iii. 20.

A HAND is on the latch,
   A foot is at the door;
A pleading voice entreats
To cross the threshold o'er;
    But awful words
    Resound within:
    "Pass on, nor break
    The dream of sin."

Is it the evening breeze
That wanders softly by?
Or was that whispered moan
A deep soul-breathèd sigh?
    The hour is late,
    The dews are chill,
    But yonder feet
    How patient still!

Beside the lintel yet,
Though all unbid to stay!
What urgent business binds?
What tokens, stranger, say?
    "My love compels:
    For tokens, see
    The scars I gained
    On yonder tree.

" Behold, I stand and knock ;
I may not knock for long ;
The flying moments haste,
But love is deep and strong.
　　Once more I knock,
　　Once more I pray :
　　Man ! wilt thou turn
　　Thy God away ? "

And then a Hand is raised,
It bears a wan, deep scar ;
Back roll the stubborn bolts,
Down falls each ponderous bar.
　　The door is moved,
　　It shifts its place :
　　The twain are standing
　　Face to face.

No words, but with a smile
He goes at once within,
Amidst the shades and gloom,
In spite of stain and sin.
　　And lit by love
　　And power divine,
　　The darkened hearth
　　Becomes a shrine.

WHILE THE EMBERS GLOW.

"God requireth that which is past."—*Eccles.* iii. 15.

WHEN the curtains of the twilight
  Close around us one by one,
While the deepening shadows whisper
  That the toils of day are done,
Then our thoughts seem purer, clearer
  Than, alas! they often are,
Brightening, as they draw the nearer
  To the land beheld afar;
Then reflection gladly wanders
  From the daily toil and strife,
As the musing spirit ponders
  On the fallen sands of life.

As we slowly turn the pages
  Of our changeful days and years,
Oh, how many leaves are sullied,
  Blotted with repentant tears!
Oh, how few there are whose whiteness
  Uncondemned may meet the eye!
Oh, how few there are whose brightness
  Must not lose by scrutiny!
Soiled' and tarnished, marred and clouded,
  All their light and glory gone;
Strangely mingled are our musings,
  As we search them, one by one.

Yet, amidst our self-wrought sorrows,
　Nature teacheth holy things:
What a gentle placid glory
　Goes through all her communings!
Still along life's chequered pathway
　Varied lights and shadows play,
And to-day some eyes are smiling
　Through the tears of yesterday.
Not for ever lasts the weeping,
　Not in vain our hearts well o'er;
E'en the very waves of anguish
　Waft us to a brighter shore.

Just a little nearer heaven
　Day by day we trust we are;
Just a very little closer
　To the coast that seems so far;
Just a little less of sinning,
　Fewer clouds to fleck the sky;
Just a little nearer winning
　The eternal victory;
Just a very little purer,
　Cleansed from some defiling blot;
Just, we hope, a little surer
　Of the crown that fadeth not.

Day by day, perhaps, our footsteps
　Falter in the weary road;
Yet each print is leading upwards
　To the Paradise of God;
To the house of many mansions,
　To the kingdom of the blest,
Where the wicked cease from troubling,
　Where the weary are at rest.

DOMUM, DULCE DOMUM!

In My Father's house are many mansions."—*St. John* xiv. 2.

BEYOND the changeful splendours
  Where west winds softly play,
And wave the dappled curtains
  Which fringe the far-away,
The "house of many mansions"
  Lifts up its fair array.

Beyond life's restless surges
  The crystal sea gleams bright,
And there the strings are sounding
  Which radiant harpers smite,
Where now the saved are walking
  In sheeny robes of white.

The lambent air is gleaming
  With angels' lustrous wings,
And there are eyes that gaze on
  A thousand glorious things,
The outskirts of the splendour
  Which veils the King of kings.

And there are voices singing
  The other side that sea ;
But here, ah ! no man showeth
  How sweet those songs may be :
The echoes of that music
  Sound in an unknown key.

But still beyond our sorrows,
  So sad, so hard to bear,
Are fresh and bright to-morrows
  Which wait us over there,
And ah ! to those who journey,
  That far-off home is fair.

Beyond the yellow sunsets
  Which streak the storm-tossed main,
The golden gates are gleaming
  Through all the mist and rain ;
And none whose feet may win them
  Shall feel the storms again.

INTERCESSION.

"Pray for one another."—*St. James* v. 16.

PRAY for one another :
　　Surely we might bear
More each other's burdens
　　On the wings of prayer.
Many a trembling teardrop
　　Might be wiped away,
If the friends who loved us
　　Did but kneel and pray.

Pray for one another :
　　If we did but know
Prayers were hovering round us
　　Wheresoe'er we go,
Death would lose its shadows ;
　　Life would lose its cares,
Were we more supported
　　By our loved ones' prayers.

Pray for one another :
　　Jesus prays for you ;
Follow those dear footsteps,
　　Pray for others too.
Think how, hanging anguished
　　On that cross, He cried,
"Father, O forgive them !"
　　Just before He died.

Pray for one another :
　Well we need these prayers,
'Midst our toils and strivings,
　'Midst our fears and cares ;
Many a heart were lighter,
　Many a tear were dry,
Many a robe were whiter,
　Did they scale the sky.

Pray for one another :
　Keep that sacred tryst,
" Bear each other's burdens "
　To the feet of Christ.
Plead we each for other
　Through the little while,
Till our upturned faces
　Catch the angels' smile.

SHADOWS ON THE WALL.

the day break, and the shadows flee away."—*Cant.* ii. 17.

WHEN the light is softly waning,
   Comes a time for thought and prayer,
While the soul unbinds the burden
   Of her daily cross and care.

Then, amidst the ghostly shadows
   Flickering faintly on the floor,
Memory with her tender fingers
   Turns life's pages o'er and o'er,

Bringing back the vanished sunshine,
   Bringing back the childish mirth ;
Echoes soft as angel footsteps
   Sound once more again on earth.

Tones whose gentle winning pleadings
   Never may be quite forgot,
Though the loving lips that spoke them
   Slumber on and answer not.

Day by day the cross grows lighter,
   While we keep our evening tryst,
Kneeling softly in the twilight
   At the gentle feet of Christ.

Some we miss are lying silent,
　With their feet towards the east,
Waiting till the day-star rising
　Call them to the bridal feast.

And we too in faith are waiting,
　Though our faith be mixed with pain,
Till the dead who sleep in Jesus
　Shall be given us back again,—

Given back in life and beauty,
　Given back in deed and truth,
In their resurrection garments,
　Radiant with eternal youth.

All we loved in them expanded,
　All the reunited ties
Knit again to last for ever,
　With their tender sympathies.

Oh the holy raptured greetings
　That shall thrill yon fragrant air!
Oh the blessed words of welcome
　Waiting wanderers over there!

Oh how silver sweet the voices!
　Oh how fair the features grown!
"Changed from glory into glory,"
　Changed, but still our own, our own.

As the light is softly waning,
　And we kneel awhile in prayer,
Upwards, like the clouds of incense,
　Float our thoughts to meet them there.

Sweet it is to pass a moment
  Thus beyond our sighs and tears,
Past the sad reproachful voices
  Of the wistful weary years!

Sweet to close the eyes, while fancy,
  Soaring through these changeful skies,
Basks awhile in yonder regions
  Warm with tints of Paradise,

Treads awhile the golden pathway,
  Wanders by the crystal sea,
In the far-off deathless splendour
  Of that glory that shall be

When these fleeting earthly sunsets
  Shall be lost in fadeless day,
When the former things of sorrow
  Pass for evermore away!

ALTA QUIES.

" He giveth His beloved sleep."—Psalm cxxvii.

A FEW more nights of languor,
　　A few more days of pain,
A few more pulses' beatings
　And throbbings of the brain;
A few more sins and sorrows,
　A few more falls and fears,
A few to-days, to-morrows;
　And then an end to tears.
For Jesus, the Good Shepherd,
　Shall claim His wandering sheep:
He giveth His beloved
　The quiet gift of sleep.

A little more of conflict,
　Although perhaps my share,
Instead of active service,
　May only be to bear;
A little farther onwards
　The burden must be borne;
Night lasts a little longer,
　And then the streaks of morn.
Then He, the great Good Shepherd
　Shall claim His wandering sheep,
And give to His beloved
　The quiet gift of sleep.

Oh, sweet, at early morning,
  To watch the golden sun
Light up the silent valleys
  With glory, one by one.
Or sweeter still at even,
  To seaward, when the light
Gleams like the gates of heaven,
  So jasper-clear and bright.
But oh ! when white-winged angels
  Shall throw those gates aside,
And call within their portals
  The souls for whom He died,—
When He, their own Good Shepherd,
  Shall claim each wandering sheep,
And give to His beloved
  The quiet gift of sleep.

For me the morn is breaking,
  Light floodeth all the vale,
The gentle hands that hold me
  I know can never fail.
And though my sun be setting
  Like evening in the west,
The ocean where it hideth
  Is this—the Saviour's breast.
And Jesus, the Good Shepherd,
  Shall claim His wandering sheep.
He giveth His beloved
  The quiet gift of sleep.

ANASTASIS.

"From glory to glory."—2 *Cor*. iii. 18.

WHAT strange sights shall meet our eyes
    When they wake beyond the skies!
Splendour past our best surmising,
At that mighty re-arising;
When our long-lost loved ones greet us,
When the dead in Christ shall meet us,
While the startled air is bright,
Trembling with excess of light.

What slight fetters hold us here!
Time how short may take us there,—
Take us from this land of sorrow
To that ever bright to-morrow.
One breath wanting, only one,
And we stand beyond the sun,
Finding with that failing breath
Life begin to live in death.

Soon beyond the rolling hours,
Past the sunlight and the showers,
Free from links of earth that bound us,
With those spells life wove around us.
Just one strange electric shiver,
And we stand beyond the river;
In that moment snatched from time
Life begins to be sublime.

Soon within the narrow bound
Of some unremembered mound,
Anxious aim and high endeavour
Lie at rest—at rest for ever.
Offsprings of the fever'd brain
Passed to nothingness again,
While our earthy mother's breast
Hides her earthy children's rest.

Then the scales of flesh shall fall
From the eyes they held in thrall,
As the spirit's powers expand
In the mystic spirit-land.
With our feet beyond the portal
Of the broadening life immortal,
What eternal progress waits,
Through and past the golden gates!

Round that cross to which we cling
Brightens an eternal spring:
Oh to touch with tightening clasp!
Oh to hold with firmer grasp!
Whiter garments here to wear,
Till we gain the vesture there,
In that solemn hour when we
Sail on yonder shoreless sea!

THROUGH THE RIFTS.

" The blue sky bends over all."— Christabel.

THE dreary mist is cold and grey,
    The gentle rain begins to fall,
But not so very far away
    The blue sky bendeth over all.

Though dark the rolling drift appears,
    And bitter sweets that turn to gall,
Yet could we pass beyond our fears,
    The blue sky bendeth over all.

Some eyes with wistful tears are wet,
    And grief holds many a heart in thrall,
For time and death are strong—but yet
    The blue sky bendeth over all.

When through the parting clouds of care,
    Our ears shall catch the angels' call,
How sweet to reach the regions where
    The blue sky bendeth over all!—

When all the sharpest pangs are past,
    As pain itself begins to pall,
To find in God's own peace at last,
    The blue sky bending over all!

AN UNKNOWN GRAVE.

"Thou shalt stand in thy lot at the end of the days."—
Dan. xii. 13.

THERE is a little plot of ground,
　Though where I cannot tell,
But yet within its shelt'ring calm
　I think to slumber well.
The sun shall shine, the sun shall set,
　The shadows rise and fall,
While I shall lie there, hushed and still,
　At peace beyond them all.

Perhaps amid the bright green fields
　This unknown spot may lie,
Where some grey village spire uplifts
　The cross towards the sky;
Or else within the busy haunts
　Of toiling, striving men,
The trampling of whose restless feet
　Will not disturb me then.

The pleasant breath of early spring
　May touch this plot of ground,
Or autumn, with her golden sheaves,
　May spread her tints around,

Or wintry clouds may hide the sky,
　And tempest's voice may roar;
But I shall be beyond the reach
　Of storm for evermore.

The matins of the joyous lark,
　The thrush's evensong,
The whispering of the twilight breeze,—
　These sounds shall steal along;
And when the midnight bells ring out,
　In tones so sweet and clear,
The chimings of the better land
　Shall sound within mine ear.

*　　　*　　　*　　　*

There is a spot,—it is on high,
　I cannot tell you where;
But oh! 'tis in the light of God,
　And Jesus will be there;
I cannot say how bright it is,
　Or how its glories shine,
But it has been prepared for me,
　And some day shall be mine,—

My very own for evermore:
　For time, and sin, and death
Have never touched this blessed spot
　With their polluting breath.
The sands of time are wet with tears,
　But those dear shores are bright;
These toilworn feet shall tread them soon,
　'Mid resurrection light.

I cannot tell what gentle eyes
  From thence are·gazing now;
I cannot tell what rainbow hues
  Throw halos round the brow;
I may not know what accents make
  Soft music on that air,
Till time and tears and death are done,
  And I myself am there.

But yet, sweet home in Paradise,
  I greet thee from afar;
Safe in thy calm unruffled peace,
  The dead in Jesus are.
Fair harbour o'er the stormy sea,
  How bright thy light appears!
Although we sometimes catch thy gleams
  Behind a rain of tears.

COMFORT.

"As thy days so shall thy strength be."—Deut. xxxiii. 35.

WHEN in sorrow's furnace tried,
    Lean thee on the Crucified ;
When thy heart is sore dismayed,
Wrestle on, nor be afraid :
Listen, this is writ for thee,—
" As thy day, thy strength shall be."

When thine eyes with tears are wet,
Then remember Olivet !
Know that He who, prostrate there,
Poured away His soul in prayer,
Counts thy pangs and notes thy sighs,
Though He reigns beyond the skies.

If beneath the curtains white
Thou must wake the weary night,
While the awful fangs of pain
Fasten on the shrinking brain,
Still abides the firm decree—
" As thy day, thy strength shall be."

When the morning's wished-for gleams
Wake thy fitful, fever'd dreams,
And the daily cross appears
Looming through a mist of tears,
Turn thy weary heart aside :
Rest thee on the Crucified.

By each anguished throb and throe
Borne so meekly years ago,
By the gentle hands outspread,
By the patient thorn-crowned head,
Kneel at yonder nail-pierced feet,
Till the bitter cup grow sweet.

Take the comfort there bestowed :
It will lighten all thy load ;
Succours sought and surely given,
Smooth the weary way to heaven.
Know that this was writ for thee,—
"As thy day, thy strength shall be."

When with features drawn and pale,
Thou must dare the darksome vale
As the closing eyelid falls,
'Tis the voice of Jesus calls :
"Parting soul, arise, be free!
As thy day, thy strength shall be."

PRESSING TOWARD THE MARK.

"Faint, yet pursuing them."—*Judges* viii. 4.

I'M faint, but yet pursuing;
　Far off my home appears;
Sometimes its lights shine dimly
　Behind a veil of tears;
But be it midday splendour,
　Or drear beclouded noon,
'Mid shine or storm or shadow,
　I'm slowly wrestling on.

Sometimes the way seems rugged,
　Sometimes the path is sweet,—
Some steps must aye be trodden
　With wearied, bleeding feet;
But be it smoothed with mercies,
　Or rough with thorn and stone,
Each step is one step nearer,
　And so I'm journeying on.

It is not always Marah,
　Not always desert ground,
But Elims with their palm-trees
　Are ofttimes gladly found.
And as in Israel's wanderings,
　Where'er the pillar shone,
The tribes might safely travel,
　'Tis thus I'm journeying on.

My footsteps are but feeble,
  And sometimes leave the track,
But One whose eyes are on me
  In mercy leads me back.
Deep stains are on my garments,
  But till those stains are gone,
In spite of falls and failures
  I'm slowly wrestling on.

Some who once trod beside me
  Have passed me in the race;
They wait within the shelter
  Of yonder meeting-place.
Their ship has made the harbour,
  Their storms are past and gone;
Yet, 'mid the waves and tempests,
  I still am struggling on.

What steps must yet be taken
  'Tis not for me to say,—
Perhaps the journey's ending
  Is not so far away;
But be it just before me,
  Or in long years to come,
May each step take me nearer
  To Christ, and rest, and home!

SOON

"A little while."—*Heb.* x. 37.

OH, what wilt thou be soon,
    O fluttering soul of mine?
A little while, and thou must pass
Beyond the bounds of time.
        Life's sands are falling
        One by one,
        But what when all
        Those sands are done?

I shall be sinless soon:
Oh high majestic joy—
A heart that only beats for God,
And knows not sin's alloy!
        A stainless robe,
        A soul all pure,
        And thoughts all white
        For evermore.

I shall be tearless soon;
Now each day brings its pain,
But soon these wistful weary eyes
Shall never weep again.
        O mortal grief,
        How short thy sway,
        Ere God shall wipe
        All tears away!

I shall be deathless soon:
To-morrow's sun shall rise,
Yet I, or e'er it sets, may be
  Beyond its purpled skies.
        O truer life—
        Eternity—
        How soon my soul
        May dwell with thee!

I shall be glorious soon:
My face is lined by care,
But you shall search these features o'er
  In vain for sorrow there.
        Soon shall each stain
        Be cast aside—
        I, like my Master,
        Glorified.

I shall see angels soon—
Those elder sons of light—
And gaze upon each awful face,
  Unutterably bright.
        How soon those pure
        Benignant eyes
        May welcome speak
        To Paradise!

And I shall soon behold
The dear ones of the past,
The friends who died long years ago,
  And those I loved the last:
        In Jesus they
        Sleep one by one,
        And I in Him
        Shall slumber soon.

I shall see Jesus soon,
And here all words must cease,
His gaze will fill this throbbing heart
With deep unchanging peace.
    For e'en on earth
    The little while
    Is lighted by
    His tender smile.

THE OTHER SIDE.

"The land that is very far off."--*Isa.* xxxiii. 17.

JUST beyond the river,
　　Oh how sweet and pure,
Is the peace that circles
　　All the sinless shore!
Never sigh or sadness
　　Wounds the gentle air,
Only words of gladness
　　Make the language there.

Just beyond the river,
　　What a welcome waits
Those who once but enter
　　Through the shining gates!
What dear eyes may glisten
　　In that distant home!
What quick ears may listen
　　Till each loved one come!

Just beyond the river
　　Childish feet have trod,
Wafted o'er the waters
　　To the peace of God.
In the regions yonder
　　What a fadeless glow
Circles with its wonder
　　Many an infant brow!

Just beyond the river
　　Voices we may hear,—
Tones for which we've wearied
　　Many and many a year!
Lips we kissed so sadly
　　In those tearful days
There are parted gladly
　　In the strain of praise.

Just beyond the river
　　Glows immortal light;
While we watch and wonder,
　　All the strand is bright:
See, the tints are streaming
　　Through the trembling air;
Flashing forms are gleaming
　　'Mid the glories there.

Just beyond the river
　　There is One who stands
With the nail-prints written
　　In His tender hands,—
One whose voice is calling,
　　"Weary wanderers, come!"
Yes, those sweet words, falling,
　　Float across the foam.

Just beyond the river
　　There is room for you:
Will you reach those regions
　　Jesus asks you to?
Are your sins as scarlet?
　　He is one, you know,
Who can wash those garments
　　Whiter than the snow.

Just beyond the river,
  Or to gain or loss,
In a few swift seasons
  One by one we cross:
Though we shrink and shiver,
  As we face the tide,
Just beyond the river
  Lies the brightest side.

DE PROFUNDIS.

"In the hour of death and in the day of judgment, good deliver us."—*Litany*.

As day by day the lessening thread
Of life frays out its golden strands,
Our hours are numbered with the dead,
Our glass is filled with fallen sands.

The vessel speeds with flashing keel,
And bears the buffets of the waves;
But soon the quivering ship must reel
On yonder shore all thick with graves.

The warmest blood must lose its heat,
The surest feet go down the hill,
The strongest pulse must cease to beat,
And all the stormy heart be still.

Our eyes are wet with wistful tears,
Our brows are bent with brooding thought;
We scan our sheaf of changeful years,
And all our musings come to nought.

The air is filled with taunting cries,
The bitter cup o'erflows the brim;
The gloom of death is in the skies,
And all the shining shore is dim.

Oh, mighty strength that cannot fail,
Oh, love that knowest how and why,
In pity stoop and rend the veil,
And tell us what it is to die!

We hear those awful accents call
Our lives that wander to and fro,
But let some gleams of sunshine fall
Amid the shadows as we go.

Oh, gentle hands that hold the cross
Before the glazing eye in death,
Let gain be perfected in loss,
And strengthen all the cords of faith.

The tangled riddles all unread,
The things too hard to understand,
The mysteries that time has bred,
We leave within that nail-pierced Hand.

For love can read the scroll aright,
The bitter cross can give the key,—
From Calvary there streams a light
That flashes o'er the shoreless sea.

THE LAND BEYOND THE SEA.

"Homesick we are for thee,
  Calm land beyond the sea!"—*Faber.*

BEYOND the sunset, far away,
    Beyond the heather-tinted lea,
There glows a country strangely sweet,
A land that lies beyond the sea.

Beyond the crests which rise and fall,
Past clouds whose purple pales to grey,
Outstretch those shores more bright than
Fair shores that shine so far away!

The sun may set in crimson haze,
His dying splendours streak the tide,
But yet no shades of evening dim
The brightness of that further side.

And while the drifting cloud-wrack falls,
As breakers thunder on the shore,
The feet that tread yon golden sands
Have done with storms for evermore.

Anon, when ocean's breast is hushed,
As daybreak waketh fresh and fair,
No sunlight tints those far-off hills,
'Tis everlasting morning there.

The wistful eyes are over there:
Tears dimmed them oft this side the sea;
But in the land they gaze on now
Nor sorrowing nor sigh can be.

The weary feet are over there,
Which here were often pained and sore,
But now they tread those peaceful shores,
And shall feel weary never more.

The loving hands are over there:
Of friends, the trusted and the tried,
And they shall grasp our own ere long,
When we ourselves have passed the tide.

The quiet hearts are over there:
Here ofttimes throbbed each fluttering breast;
But now eternal peace is theirs
Within that better land of rest.

Beyond the mists which float and rise,
And fill this sorrow-laden air,
Outstretch the ever cloudless skies
Of that dear country over there.

Like some tired mariner, whose bark
Drops anchor where he fain would be,
May we, when strife and storm are past,
Reach that fair land beyond the sea!

THE VIGIL.

"Let me go, for the day breaketh."—*Gen*. xxxii. 26.

JESUS each night is watching
   Beside each sufferer's bed;
Oft as the shadows darken
   Around each aching head,
He notes those weary tossings
   Which seek for rest in vain,
And whispereth, "In heaven
   There shall be no more pain."

Oh, some of His lie wakeful
   On beds as soft as down,
And some on hard rough pallets
   In country or in town;
But yet there's One who's watching
   Where'er His people lie,—
Amid the shadows, Jesus
   Is surely standing by.

The gold without the furnace
   Were else all dulled and dim;
Some hearts alone by anguish
   Grow fit and meet for Him.
Our souls shrink back in weakness
   When first the flames they view,
But we forget that Jesus
   Walks 'mid the burning too.

In many a far-off chamber,
  Though hid from mortal sight,
The gleaming angel pinions
  Are folded soft to-night.
And feet that halt and tremble
  With fear to stem the tide
Will pass the waters safely
  If Jesus stand beside.

Far in the east the starlight
  Grows faint and fainter still,
As gleams that tell of daybreak
  Creep up the window-sill.
The lattices are shaking,
  A soft wind moves the door,
And lo! the watching angels
  Spread wide their wings once more.

A shout of welcome yonder,
  A wail from earth below—
The disembodied spirits
  Float on the sunrise glow.
In many an earthly chamber
  The salt, salt tears well o'er,
But the house of many mansions
  Is fuller than before.

SHADOW-LAND.

" Until the day break and the shadows flee away."—*Cant.* ii.

EACH heart has a haunted room,
    Where, amidst the hallowed gloom,
Deep within its shelter laid,
Dwell the memories of the dead.
Sometimes in the twilight hours
Shadowy lips seem pressed to ours;
Sometimes near th' unconscious head
Footsteps all unearthly tread.
Palms that in the years ago
Sought our own in weal or woe,
Towards us stretch with waving hand
From that death-divided strand
Accents strangely sweet and clear,
Silent many and many year,
In and out the wearied brain
Wander like a soft refrain;
As the tones which gently sound
Fall and float on holy ground.
Ah! this chamber in the breast
Harbours many a longed-for guest:
Some are young, and some are old;
Some lie pale beneath the mould:
Yet within this chamber door
We can meet them all once more.

Little hands so soft and clinging,
Little voices blithe and ringing,
Brows all bright with manhood's glory,
Brows so patient, seamed, and hoary.
Lips on which the turf has lain
Whisper kindly words again;
Eyes that scan yon angel bowers
Turn once more to answer ours;
Feet the waves of death have wet
Turn and walk beside us yet.
While they in this chamber tread,
We may hardly deem them dead.
Called to earth from shadow-land,
Fresh and beautiful they stand:
Buds that withered years ago
Seem once more to bloom and blow;
Hopes so sweet they faded fast,
Ere the morning's dews were past—
Hopes perchance to blossom still
In the land invisible.
Seeds we watered oft with tears
Yield in those eternal years
An unshaded world of bliss,
Sought, but vainly sought, in this.
Here on earth they had their root,
There beyond they bear their fruit;
Here the sowing and the weeping,
There the harvest-tide and reaping:
Here they faded like the leaves,
There the Master binds the sheaves.
Yes, this chamber in the breast
Glows with many a wondrous guest,
Tender gleams and glints that come
From the many-mansioned home.

EVENTIDE.

"At evening time it shall be light."—*Zech.* xiv. 7.

AS the day's declining gleams
 Fall upon some tree or tower,
Increase of each beauty seems
Yielded in that fleeting hour.

When the summer's splendour fades,
Ere the wintry blasts are near,
With what witching tints and shades
Does the autumn gold appear!

When the strains of music die,
Ere the soaring echoes fall,
How the latest soft-breathed sigh
Seems the sweetest of them all!

When we bend, all succour past,
Over lips so pale and dead,
How the tones that thrilled them last
Seem the dearest words they said!

When the beating clock of Time
Points to midnight with its hands,
How the straining woof of life
Woven seems with golden strands!

When asleep on Jesus' breast
Sinks the Christian's wearied brow,
Gleams from yon celestial hills
Spread around a fadeless glow.

Calm upon the quiet eyes,
Rest upon the forehead fair:
Those who scan the wasted face
Feel the peace of God is there.

REUNION.

"I shall go to him, but he shall not return to me."—
2 *Sam.* xii. 23.

MET again to part no more,
    After all the weary years ;
Met again, the weeping o'er,
After all the scalding tears,—

After sin's delusive snares,
After struggles, hopes, and sighs ;
After sorrows calmed by prayers,
Met again, in Paradise.

Met again in fullest light,
"Heart to heart, and hand to hand,"
After wanderings in the night,
Wanderings God can understand.

After all the smiles and tears,
After all the hushed, low prayers ;
After all the hopes and fears,
Life's bewildering, blinding cares.

Met within that Presence high,
Where our chains are cast aside
By the strength that stooped to die,
To be scourged and crucified.

In His presence evermore
Who has burst sin's galling bands,
Torn from death the sting it bore,
Writ our names upon His hands.

Here all minor chords shall die,
Life's weird notes so sad and dreary,—
" Jubilates ". now on high
Take the place of " Miserere."

THE MORNING WATCH.

"Until the day break, and the shadows flee away."— *Cant.* i. 17.

A SILVER shield in sapphire set
 Upon the lone, lone sea :
The charmèd moon, with drowsy spell,
 Sheds splendour dreamily ;
A trembling pathway o'er the tide,
 Her faint, sweet light is led,
Like that wan, wistful beauty lent
 The features of the dead.

The soft white scud goes floating by,
 Like some bright, fleecy veil,
In which the haughty moon has wrapped
 Her fair, proud face so pale.
And sadly sweet the chill light falls,
 'Mid clouds like drifting snow,
Or gleams of awful radiance flashed
 From fallen angels' brow.

And far away the noiseless ships
 Go sailing to and fro,
Their spectral shrouds all ghostly white
 Beneath the moonlit glow.
While on the gleaming wet sea-sand,
 With measured, echoing moan,
The weird eternal ocean rolls
 Its strange, deep undertone.

O summer sea, sweet summer sea !
  Thy spell is deep and lone ;
The surges on thy silver sands
  Fall flashing, one by one.
Yet, could I claim the seabird's wing,
  And climb yon radiant stair,
My baffled hope and heart must find
  But disappointment there.

Soon, like some hues of Paradise
  Faint in the purple east,
The "roseate tints of dewy morn"
  Will blush on ocean's breast;
But when shall that dear morning come,
  The answer to her tears,
Which this sad earth has wearied for
  Full eighteen hundred years ?

PART. II.

RIGHI SUNSET.

'Until the day break, and the shadows flee away."— *Cant.* ii. 17.

S OFT light upon the Righi,
   Upon the lakes below ;
The witching, transient, roseate tints
   Which Alpine sunsets know.
Mountains in purple glory,
   Dark valleys robed in grey,
Red streaks and gleams of splendour,—
   But all to pass away.

Soft light upon the Righi,
   Clouds edged with crimson fire,
Red bars with orange blending
   Each flickering lance and spire ;
A thousand shapes of beauty,
   A thousand tints and glows,
And like some angel's robe on earth
   Those far-off Alpine snows.

Soft light upon the Righi,
   Though fair thy sun and shine,
Yet earth shall know a fairer scene,
   A splendour passing thine.
Though gemmed with light and beauty,
   Lucerne, thy wavelets be,
Yet what their flashing brightness
   To thine, O crystal sea ?

Oh, brighter than the "Glarnisch,"
　　With all its silvery sheen,
The land no stain can tarnish,
　　Which eye hath not yet seen!
Soft light upon the Righi,
　　How fair thy roseate skies!
But oh the fadeless, deathless glow
　　That circles Paradise!

THE NAME IN SAND.

"But rather rejoice because your names are written in heaven."—
St. Luke x. 20.

I WROTE a name upon the sand,
  Beside the moaning surf;
'Twas but the empty name of one
  Long silent 'neath the turf.
I watched the rippling, laughing waves
  Break softly on the shore;
But love and life looked desolate,—
  My heart was sad and sore.

'Twas sunset on the purple sea;
  I watched that thrice-loved name,
As far to westward sank the light
  In one broad blaze of flame;
While near and nearer crept the tide,
  Until at last, effaced,
That name that was the world to me
  Lay blotted and erased.

"Ah! thus," thought I, "Eternity
  Blots out Time's golden sands;
The waves of that tremendous sea
  Part hopes and hearts and hands."
But from the westward then there flashed
  A ray so pure and sweet:
A message from that far-off shore
  Was lying at my feet.

A message without voice, and yet
　I knew its meaning well;
For Nature sometimes writes her thoughts
　Too deep for words to tell;
And in that opal-tinted streak,
　That flashed across the sea,
God's finger, tipped with living light,
　Was writing words for me.

"In vain," it said, "thy love would strive
　To write that name in sand;
'Tis graven in the roll of those
　Who tread the deathless land.
And thou, whene'er thy heart is sad,
　When life seems hard to bear,
Then think of that dear, far-off home,
　And one who waits thee there."

Long years ago, long years ago,
　Those streaks of splendour died,
Like tresses which the golden sun
　Trailed o'er the shimmering tide.
But still, whene'er that tender light
　Glows over shore and lea,
I think of that sweet message flashed
　That evening o'er the sea.

THE BROKEN FLOWER.

'' He shall carry the lambs in His bosom."—*Isa.* xl. 11.

OH, bind her hair with roses,
    Wreathe clusters o'er that brow ;
The sleep where death reposes
    Has mantled o'er its snow;
And joy, and pride, and sorrow
    Have died from out those eyes,—
Which gaze on Life's to-morrow,
    And see in Paradise.

The things we dare not fathom,
    The thoughts we may not know,
In all their perfect beauty
    Our darling knoweth now.
No dream of sorrow darkling
    May cloud the eye of faith,
For shade is lost in lustre,
    And life begins in death.

Her hands are meekly folded
    Across her gentle breast,
Her fingers twined for ever
    For one unbroken rest.
And in a dreamless slumber,
    With marbled brow and chill,
She lieth, veiled in silence,
    And passionless and still.

The white rose nestles softly
  Beside that cold, cold cheek,
Which lieth pale and changeless,
  So wan, and pure, and meek.
The myrtle's spray is peeping
  From out that golden hair,
But ah! the fairest floweret
  Lies crushed and broken there,—

A flower amid the flowerets,
  A pale and broken flower,
Now sown in tearful weakness,
  Then raised in wondrous power;
Though these shall fade and wither,
  Like rosebuds on the pall,
She hears the "Come up hither,"
  And blooms beyond them all.

A lovely star has fallen
  From our terrestrial sky,
And with a blaze of beauty
  Has swept its glory by.
But oh! it gleameth brighter,
  With purer, clearer glow,
Amid the shining circlet
  That binds the thorn-crowned Brow.

LITTLE EVELYN.

"Is it well with the child?"—2 *Kings* iv. 26.

LITTLE Evelyn, where is she?
    Ask where last year's rosebuds be?
Where the songs so sweet and low
Breathed but one short hour ago?
Where the changeful opal light
Of the sunset yesternight?
Where the tints on yonder lea?
Where the hues that streaked the sea?—
Live these on, though lost to view?
Little Evelyn lives so too.

Little Evelyn, where is she?
Who knows where the angels be?
Who can say how soft the breast
Where the lambs are lulled to rest?
Who can tell how pure the flowers
Wreathing those eternal bowers,
Or how fair 'neath yonder skies
Grow the plants of Paradise?
Questions these we cannot tell:
Maybe Evelyn knows them well.

Little Evelyn, where is she?
Ask, but who shall answer thee?
Who can tell how sweet and wise
Shine those childish, wistful eyes?
Or how bright those features now,
With the rays around her brow?
Who may say what raiment white
Wraps those tender limbs to-night?
Love and grief are hushed; I wist,
Little Evelyn is with Christ.

A MOTHER'S ARMS.

(FOUNDED UPON A WELL-KNOWN STORY.)

" As one whom his mother comforteth."—*Isa.* lxvi. 13.

A LITTLE child was dying;
    A mother watched beside;
With wistful gaze of anguish
    The blue eyes open wide.
A mother's tears were falling
    Beside that restless bed,
As all in vain she tried to soothe
    The tossing golden head.

She spoke of all the brightness
    Of that eternal place,
Where little children's angels
    Look on our Father's face;
Of all its sheeny splendour,
    Of more than rainbow skies.
" But, mother," sighed a little voice,
    " The light would hurt my eyes."

In grief she changed her story,
    And told the suffering child
What music fills those golden halls
    By sorrow undefiled—
The voice of many waters
    So rich and deep and free—
And of the white-robed harpers
    Beside the crystal sea;

Of that sweet song that ringeth
  With more than silver notes,
Of all that glad rejoicing,
  God's melody, that floats
Through all the streets of Zion,
  'Mid merry girls and boys.
But then there came a little sob:
  " I could not bear the noise."

And then, in grief and anguish,
  With salt tears blinding fast,
She took the little fevered head
  Upon her breast at last;
While from that restful shelter
  There came the whispered prayer,—
"Mother, if heaven is like this,
  May Jesus take me there!"

MARY'S VOYAGE.

"Jesus called a little child unto Him."—*St. Matt.* xviii. 2.

THREE fair-haired little maidens
Were playing by the sea
One golden summer's evening,
As blithe as blithe could be.
Their guardian angels near them
Beheld their childish glee.

Loud rang their sunny laughter,
For each in turn would dare
A raid upon old ocean,
As, wild, with tossing hair,
They chased the murmuring wavelets,
With feet all pink and bare.

Said rosy blue-eyed Una,
"I wish the stones around
Were changed to gold and silver,
As on Tom Tiddler's ground:
I'd gather handfuls of them,
And keep them, I'll be bound."

"And I," said pretty Ida,
"Wish I were rich and great,
To buy the castle yonder,
With all its fair estate;
And there I'd live in grandeur,"
Said little miss, sedate.

Said gentle, soft-eyed Mary,
  "I wonder where the sun
Can go to every evening
  As soon as day is done :
If I'd a ship, I'd follow,—
  And wouldn't that be fun ?

"The sails should each be purple,
  The seats all ivory,
The oars should all be golden,
  And you should come with me.
Then we would go a-sailing
  Across the dear old sea."

      *   *   *   *

Mary has gone a-sailing,
  But has not come again
To tell us of the country
  She found across the main,—
The everlasting sunshine,
  Beyond the mists and rain.

The sails were not all purple,
  But white and cold were they ;
The oars were not all golden,
  But soiled with mould and clay ;
And they have wafted Mary,
  Oh, somewhere far away !

Mary has gone a-sailing :
  The sunlight she may see
Is all too bright and peaceful
  For earth to bring to me.
Those little feet are resting
  The other side the sea.

FLOWERS AMID THE CORN.

"Of such is the kingdom of heaven."—*St. Matt.* xix. 14.

A BROTHER died long years ago,—
  God's glory hides him now,—
Nor sin nor pain had time to stain
  My little kinsman's brow.
Upon that childish head of down
The cross so soon became a crown; •
  How sweet its light and glow!

A little maid with gentle eyes
  Sings by a far-off sea,
And when I dream, I think they seem
  To turn and gaze on me.
When Christian children sink to rest,
They slumber on their Saviour's breast,
  And so, I know, doth she.

Long years ago, in Syrian land,
  His lips said, Ἄφετε,
Let children dear to Me draw near,
  καὶ μὴ κωλύετε:
My life for theirs is freely given,
They see My Father's face in heaven:
  τὰ παιδία ἄφετε.

Our earthly flowers amid the corn
  Have angels pure and wise,
Whose loving guard keeps watch and ward
  Before the awful eyes
Of Him whose Son, the Virgin-born,
Partook our weakness and its scorn :
  O depth of mysteries !

Perhaps in that tremendous hour,
  When, worn by years and pain,
Our eyelids close in that repose
  Which waketh not again,—
To bid us to the far-off home
The little loving feet may come,
  For which our hearts are fain.

A few swift rolling seasons here,
  How short their span appears !
And we shall press with soft caress
  The lips we've mourned for years
As round us smile the long-shut eyes
That meet our own with sweet surprise,
  Last seen through mists and tears.

O King of that dear far-off land,
  Upon whose glittering shore
The children wait within that gate
  Through which they pass no more :
Oh, grant that, purified from sin,
Our feet may each be planted in
  Thy footsteps gone before !

LUX E TENEBRIS.

"Why art thou cast down, O my soul?"—*Psalm* xlii. 5.

O WEARY heart so sad and sore,
   O eyes that tears will sometimes dim,
O toilworn feet that seek the shore
   Where those in white shall walk with Him:
The little while will soon be past,
And God's own peace be gained at last.

Amidst the thronging world ye press,
   Yet lonely oft your pulses beat;
But oh, what joy when face to face
   The gathered hosts of God shall meet!
There will be company enow
In yonder multitude, I trow.

As day by day the sun goes down,
   As night by night the darkness falls,
Ye weary for the golden sheen
   Which floods the everlasting halls;
And cry, "Oh, roll the gates aside
Which those unfading splendours hide!"

O knees that faint beneath the cross,
   O eyes that weary for the light,
O arms that hang so feebly down,
   A little longer urge the fight:
A few more strokes against the foe,
And then the rest which victors know!

How fair the sunshine after rain!
　How glad the smiles that follow tears!
But sweeter far the sacred peace
　Which waits beyond our storm-tossed years:
The cross is hard to bear to-day;
The crown is bright that shines for aye.

The strand is not so far away;
　And though the awful waves may fall,
The vessel, spite of storm and spray,
　Shall reach the haven after all;
The harbour bar will soon be passed,
And anchorage be gained at last.

THE EVERLASTING SHORE.

"The land that is very far off."—*Isa.* xxxiii. 17.

SOME notes of my heart's music
 Are hushed for evermore,
They have floated past the river
 To the everlasting shore.

They have crossed the restless torrents
 Of the turbid stream of time;
But they sound beyond the waters
 With measured dulcet chime.

Some flowers, so wan and drooping,
 I thought they wholly died,
Are blooming fresh and radiant
 Across the swollen tide.

Some lightsome feet whose echoes
 I thought were hushed and dead
Now throng those far-off portals
 Where saints and angels tread.

Soft hands whose loving pressure
 Once soothed each restless mood
May yet enfold my fingers
 Beyond the rolling flood.

Dear lips, whose pallid beauty
  Like faded rosebuds lies,
May yet pronounce my welcome
  Where nothing lovely dies;

And gentle eyes whose glances
  Lie veiled and hushed in night
Shall look once more upon me
  In resurrection light.

The shattered hopes I cherished,
  The thoughts once fresh and free,
Are only garnered yonder,
  The other side the sea.

There are some notes whose sweetness
  Must die away in pain,
And some whose tender gladness
  May not return again.

And though on earth their music
  Be heard, alas! no more,
It has floated o'er the river
  To the everlasting shore.

A CHILD'S MATINS.

My voice shalt thou hear in the morning, O Lord."—*Psalm* v. 3.

ALL in the morning's golden sun
   I kneel me down in prayer,
And thank Thee that Thy tender love
   Hath made the world so fair.
As Thou hast kept me through the night,
So guard me in the hours of light.

With folded hands and bended knee
   A little maiden calls;
O Father, let her voice approach
   Thine everlasting halls.
Thou hear'st the ravens when they cry,
And dearer to Thine heart am I.

My body guard from hurt and pain,
   My soul from soil of sin;
Oh! let no seeds of evil rest
   My childish heart within.
May pride and anger take their flight,
And e'en my very thoughts be white.

Let Thy sweet love compassionate
   Reach all for whom I pray :—
My father and my mother bless,
   Both this and every day ;

My brothers and my sisters dear,
And all I love both far and near.

A little maiden, in the light
  Of this sweet summer morn
I kneel, and know Thou wilt not treat
  My simple cry with scorn ;
For while I plead and ask Thy grace,
The children's angels see Thy face.

And so, for His dear sake who died
  Such long, long years ago,
A little trustful maiden kneels
  In this fair sunrise glow :
O Father, keep her good and pure
Until the sunlight fades no more.

A CHILD'S EVENSONG.

"The shadows of evening are stretched out."—*Jer.* vi. 4.

A LITTLE maiden at Thy feet,
　　I bend my knees in prayer,
And plead that Thou, for Jesus' sake,
　　Wilt keep me in Thy care:
But ere the gloom of night begins
I ask forgiveness for my sins:—

For all that I have said or done
　　That has been wrong and bad,
For all the vain and idle thoughts
　　My childish heart has had,
Father, forgive Thy little lamb,
And make me holier than I am.

My father and my mother bless,
　　Those whom I love so well;
My brothers and my sisters dear,
　　And all with whom I dwell.
O heavenly Father, keep them all,
And let no evil hap befall.

A little maiden at Thy feet,
　　Before Thy throne I fall;
I open wide my childish heart
　　And simply tell Thee all:

Secure that Thou wilt deign to bless
Thy little handmaid's trustfulness.

So now, for His dear sake who died
   That I might die to sin,
Who opened wide the golden gates
   That I might enter in,
Father, preserve Thy little child,
And keep her good and undefiled.

NEW YEAR'S MORNING.

" Behold I make all things new."—*Rev.* xxi. 5.

OLD Father Time is resting
　　His scythe beside the door,
As he crieth, " Little children,
　I bring you one year more,
A gift all white and sinless,—
　But when I come again,
I shall find some marks upon it,
　Some trace of toil and stain.
Yet take this year and keep it
　As white as best you may,
Till I claim it for my Master
　When next I pass this way."

Old Father Time is shaking
　His glass beside the door,
And the golden sands are falling,
　They are falling evermore.
They are falling in the daytime,
　When the sun is warm and high ;
They are falling in the midnight,
　When the stars are in the sky.
Falling, for ever falling,
　While new years come and pass,
As old Father Time is shaking
　The sands within the glass.

Old Father Time has taken
　His glass, and scythe, and all,
And the year he carrieth with him
　Is gone beyond recall,
But the bright new gift he bringeth
　Lies spread before your door :
God help you, little children,
　To keep it white and pure,
To guard it well for Jesus,
　Until you reach the place
Where little children's angels
　Behold the Father's face.

DIVERS PATHS.

I will bring the blind by a way which they know not."—*Isa.* xlii. 16.

SOME footsteps climb the mountains,
    While others tread the vale ;
On some the sunlight falleth,
    On some the sleet and hail.
These tracks, how stern and rugged !
    Those, smooth and quickly passed !
But in the golden city
    The King's ways meet at last.

Across the burning deserts
    Some pilgrim footsteps go,
While others press in silence
    The noiseless fields of snow.
With some the way is weary,
    With some it flies so fast ;
Yet in the golden city
    The King's ways meet at last.

On some, sweet voices singing
    Make music far and near ;
On some, the stones are watered
    With many and many a tear.
Some wind in shade and quiet,
    Some bear a throng so vast ;
Yet in the golden city
    The King's ways meet at last.

Some on the curling billows
    Which sweep the angry sea
Are borne towards the haven
    In which they fain would be;
Some by the softest breezes
    That wanton round the mast;
Yet in the golden city
    The King's ways meet at last.

Some in the sunset glories
    Float down the peaceful flood,
While others' toilworn footsteps
    Are tracked by tears and blood.
For each the same bright welcome,
    When voyage or march is past,
For in the golden city
    The King's ways meet at last.

Eternal hands have planned it;
    Whate'er the path, I know
It leadeth to the country
    To which I fain would go.
So, be it shine or shadow,
    Aside let fear be cast,
Since in the golden city
    The King's ways meet at last.

PAX DEI.

"With Christ, which is far better."—*Phil.* i. 23.

THEY are gone to be with Jesus,
  We cannot wish them here;
We would not dim their radiant lot
  With mortal stain or tear;
For they are folded safely
  Upon that gentle breast,
Where many a weary lamb of earth
  Has found eternal rest.

They are gone to be with Jesus,
  To be in that sweet home
Where want, and wistfulness, and pain
  Can never, never come.
Their steps are with the angels,
  'Mid paths all fair and bright,
Where never stain of sin can fall
  Like shadows on the light.

They are gone to be with Jesus,
  So who would wish them back
To tread the rugged stones that lie
  In life's uncertain track?
Their fears and falls are over,—
  Nor falls nor fears were vain,—
But who would wish those lips to taste
  The bitter cup again?

They are gone to be with Jesus;
  Ah! would that we were there!
That these so anxious hearts were hushed,
  With all their pain and care!
They rest in yonder regions:
  Oh that we too might go
To stand beside life's crystal stream,
  Where healing waters flow!

They are gone to be with Jesus;
  And when the time is best,
Those loving arms that shelter them
  Shall take us there to rest;
And we shall be with Jesus,
  Redeemed from stain and sin;
Those noiseless gates shall open wide,—
  We, too, shall enter in.

COMPASSION.

"The longsuffering of our Lord is salvation."—
2 *St. Peter* iii. 15.

THERE are some deep feelings,
   Which we scarce disclose;
Be this thought borne with them:
   There is One who knows,—

Knows our faults and failings,
   Soiling day by day;
Yet His deep compassion
   Doth not turn away.

Not to friends the dearest,
   On whose love we call,
Tell we half our vileness:
   Jesus knows it all,— .

All our stains and strivings,
   All our wants and woes:
Oh, how sweet that Jesus
   Loves us though He knows.

Oft our wayward footsteps
   Turn to leave the fold,
Yet the hands that clasp us
   Do not loose their hold.

Human love, though tender,
  Yields to years at last;
But that love we lean on
  Holdeth firm and fast.

Human eyes, though eager,
  Fail their watch to keep;
But the eyes of Jesus
  Slumber not nor sleep.

Human ears, though patient,
  Turn at last away;
But the ear we plead with
  Bendeth down for aye.

May His gentle pleadings
  Wean our hearts from ill,
As we think with wonder—
  "Jesus loves me still."

RAYS.

"The Lord knoweth the thoughts of man."—*Psalm* xciv. 11.

THEY pass in silence from the brain,
  And some are clothed in light;
Then in a·moment earth and sky
  Seem beautiful and bright.
Fair flying moments sometimes given
Make earth seem scarcely earth, but heaven
  So beautiful, so bright.

Some thoughts lie hidden deep and sure,
  Within the far recess
Of many a rugged simple heart,
  That keeps its tenderness.
Such thoughts, methinks, are ofttimes hid
Beneath some mouldering coffin lid,
  Sacred through tenderness.

A little thing may bring them forth:
  A lock of flaxen hair;
The chime of far-off village bells
  Upon the summer air;
Some old-time ballads' soft refrain,
Which pale hushed lips may ne'er again
  Breathe on that summer air.

Some thoughts lie buried in the past,
   Beneath the load of years,
And some lie hid within the breast,
   Too deep, too deep for tears.
The years may come, the years may go,
Yet undertones like these we know
   Lie all too deep for tears.

Some thoughts seem borne on angels' wings,
   Beyond the purple light
That edges, like a braid of gold,
   The soft grey robe of night.
So wild, so weird, so pure, so free,
They wander through eternity,
   Beyond earth's cloud and night.

No seraph at those sunset gates
   Guards now life's healing tree,
The crimson of those far-off clouds
   Speaketh of Calvary.
A thought may pass those golden bars,
May wing a path beyond the stars,
   Towards the crystal sea.

I hear a voice beside that sea
   I've longed to hear for years;
I see a face whose gentle light
   I last beheld through tears;
And fingers clasp mine own again,
Though o'er their touch the turf has lain,
   All wet with mourners' tears.

Thus thoughts go flashing through the soul,
    To cause the prayer, the sigh;
And earth and air and life are changed,
    I know not how, or why.
Some seem of madness, some of mirth,
And some seem far too sweet for earth,—
    God knoweth how and why.

BEHIND THE VEIL.

"It doth not yet appear what we shall be."—1 *St. John* iii. 2.

WE know not what we shall be,
　　Or what the radiant guise
In which mortality is clothed
　　When wafted to the skies;
What rays of fadeless splendour
　　May tint that wondrous shore,
Where trouble's seething stormy waves
　　Shall break and fret no more.

O kingdom of the deathless!
　　O land that holdeth all
The best, the brightest of our race!
　　The good, the beautiful,
The gentle, the true-hearted
　　For ages past have gone
To swell thy garner, where the sheaves
　　Are gathered one by one.

O kingdom of the sinless,
　　Where never stain shall be,
To soil with its corroding blot
　　The cleansed heart's purity!
What high immortal splendour
　　May wrap the raiment white,
In which thy children meet the blaze
　　Of God's eternal light!

O kingdom of the tearless,
  Where never grief or care,
Or sigh or aught that symbols pain,
  Shall wound the peaceful air!
The links once lost and broken,
  From "love's electric chain,"
Are gathered in thy perfect round,
  And all restored again.

O land without a sorrow!
  O light beyond the sun!
O day that know'st no eventide,
  Where all life's cares are done!
Fair house beyond the waters!
  Bright home of fadeless flowers!
Within thine arms lie sheltered those
  We miss with tears from ours.

We know not what we shall be;
  "It doth not yet appear,"
That wondrous garb of glory
  The dead in Christ shall wear.
Full oft with eager searchings
  Both thought and eyes grow dim;
Yet those who meet on yonder shore
  Shall be for aye "like Him."

THE NEW-MOWN HAY.

"The grass withereth, and the flower thereof falleth away
1 *St. Peter* i. 24.

BEFORE the harvest toil begins,
  While all the earth is gay,
A perfume fills the summer breeze,—
The scent of new-mown hay.

The merry music of the scythe
  The sun-burnt toilers hear,
While in the far blue heaven above
  The lark is singing clear.

The grass was green but yesterday,
  To-day its flower is low,
And softly o'er the sultry fields
  The summer breezes blow.

The cattle on a thousand hills
  Have all their meat from God;
He clothes the uplands and the vales,
  And waters all the sod.

And though the grass which waved so free,
  And wantoned in the air,
By busy hands is laid in swathes
  Till all the fields are bare,

Yet there are flowers that cannot fade
  And meads for ever green —
The peaceful pastures of the land
  No mortal eye hath seen.

And there in robes of spotless white
  The Church's children stand,
And fear no more the scythe of death
  In all that Holy Land.

Oh, fair the glory of the grass,
  That in a moment dies!
Yes, these are fair, but fairer still
  The fields of Paradise.

THE SHIPS THAT NEVER COME *l* SEA.

"And the sea gave up the dead."—*Rev.* xx. 13.

THE wind is from the sunny south,
  The tide is full and free,
The fleet is near the harbour mouth,
  The wives are on the quay;
But there are some red, tawny sails
  That never come from sea!

The nets are drying in the sun,
  The children are at play,
The boats are nearing one by one;
  But some—ah, well-a-day!
Again the clear horizon line
  Is scanned; but where are they?

A ruddy bar lies on the west;
  It might be brave men's blood—
The breeze goes sighing o'er the sea,
  To kiss the swirling flood;
But some come sailing back no more,
  The gallant and the good.

On high Trevalga's storm-swept steep
  The gull rides home to rest,

On far-off Lundy's granite crags
　　The sea-mew preens her breast;
But some true hearts are sore for those
　　That to them oft were pressed.

The white surf thunders on the crags
　　'Neath grey Tintagel's shore,
Below Saint Genny's storm-scarred brow
　　Th' Atlantic rollers pour,
And ebon rock and fleecy foam
　　Are mingling evermore.

They sailed away on summer seas
　　Towards the blood-red sun,
The gallant ships, the slender masts,
　　The tawny sails and dun—
They sailed into the golden west,
　　And all return save one,—

One keel shall never cross the "bar,"
　　Or round each frowning head—
One step on yonder gleaming sands
　　No more may lightly tread,
Till on the further shore of Time
　　The sea gives up the dead.

I gaze across the sea of life
　　With eyes all wet with tears,
And scan the surges of the past,
　　Their tossing hopes and fears;
But, oh! for all the dreams that died
　　Beneath the vanished years,—

The buoyant hopes, the high resolve,
　The clear unclouded skies,
The beatings of the long-stilled heart,
　The glance of long-shut eyes.
Ah me! for Life's so precious freight
　In fragile argosies.

The wind is from the sunny south,
　The breeze is fresh and free,
The sea-bird skims the harbour mouth,
　And crowded is the quay;
But, oh for all the gallant ships
　That never come from sea!

REFUGE.

' Hide me under the shadow of Thy wings."—*Psalm* xvii. 8.

A H ! the softest place to rest,
　　Weary heart, is Jesus' breast.
None so tender and so tried
As our Brother crucified.
Nowhere else is calm so sweet
As beneath those piercèd feet,
Which through all the paths have gone
Where we slowly wander on.

Other hearts there are a few
That are tender, brave, and true;
Other hands, perhaps, whose thrill
Makes all memory vibrate still;
Kindly voices strangely sweet,
Melodies almost complete;
But the dearest place to rest,
Wistful heart, is Jesus' breast.

For the sweetest place for prayer
Is with Jesus everywhere—
Whether in the minster high,
As the notes go rolling by,
Till the Amen's thunder falls
On the consecrated walls;

Or beside the couch of pain,
When the reeling, care-wrought brain
Feels, amidst the mists that hide,
Dumbly for the Crucified.

Oh, the brightest place of all
Is where no more shades may fall;
And the sweetest welcome given
Is that welcome kept for Heaven.
Yet before eternal day
Hush life's fitful gusts away,
Even here the heart has rest
If it hide on Jesus' breast.

Gentle hands, for which I feel,
Hold me fast in woe or weal;
Loving eyes, I dimly see,
Hide, ah, never hide from me;
Feet, that seek me day by day,
Turn not in just wrath away.
Sinner, as I am, confest,
Jesus, fold me to Thy breast.

CHILDREN BY THE SEA.

"The promise is to you and to your children."—*Acts* ii. 39.

OF all the sunlit summer sights,
 So blithesome, pure, and free,
Say, is there aught more sweet than this,
 Our children by the sea?

The ringing laugh, the wind-tossed locks,
 The eager, outstretched hands,
The dancing, twinkling, rosy feet
 That race along the sands.

O fresh young life upon the earth!
 The very air is glad;
The rippling wavelets kiss the feet
 Of little lass or lad.

And these will delve and toil to raise
 Their forts beside the main;
But, ah! our older castles, dears,
 Are never reared again!

And these have found some gleaming stones
 That sparkle with the spray.
Ah, me! for gems in after days
 Too lightly thrown away.

And those have launched their mimic boats
 From off the sunlit shore.
But ah, our older argosies
 Come sailing home no more.

Oh, little sunburnt, loving hands,
  That work with eager glee,
What will ye grasp in after years
  From out life's stormy sea?

Oh, little steps upon the sands,
  Oh, springing tireless feet,
What weary prints in far-off lands
  May make your tale complete!

Oh, little hearts that beat so high,
  How light your pulses thrill!
But ah, how passion-tossed, perchance,
  Ere ye are hushed and still.

Oh, little voices, clear and sweet,
  That sound upon the shore,
Life's music hath its minor chords
  Before your notes are o'er!

But yet for sheer unsullied bliss,
  Unflecked by cloud or care,
I know not aught more pure than this,
  The sea and children fair.

And He who made life's golden morn
  Shall guide His children home,
When other children, yet unborn,
  Shall play beside the foam.

THE END.

Printed by Házell, Watson & Viney, Ld., London and Aylesbury.

JINIFRIED:

A LEGEND OF NORTH DEVON.

By Rev. BASIL EDWARDS, M.A.,

Author of " Songs of a Parish Priest."

PRICE ONE SHILLING.

"A simple tale of love and death,
 Which shows how evermore must meet
 The thorn and flower within the wreath,
 And bitter mingle with the sweet."

(*With Frontispiece.*)

" Is a sacred poem of a high order. . . . The author deals
vith his subject in a pure and earnest way, and tells his in-
eresting story in truly poetic language."—*Bristol Times and
Mirror, Sept.* 12*th*, 1891.

" The Rev. Basil Edwards had shown by his *Songs of a
Parish Priest* that he possessed a power of writing verse of a
pleasing and attractive form. That his little volume of songs
has been appreciated is shown by the fact that a second
edition has been issued. In *Jinifried* Mr. Edwards's muse
takes a far different, if not a higher flight, speaking from a
literary standpoint. Amid wild and rocky scenes, hallowed
by the memories of childhood, he describes in picturesque
and poetic verse a thrilling legend of North Devon. . . . The
poem is charmingly written, and cannot fail to find many
admiring readers."—*Gloucestershire Chronicle, Oct.* 24*th*, 1891.

" A pretty and tenderly written poem upon the lovers, from
the pen of the Rev. Basil Edwards."—*Clifton Society, Oct.*
22*nd*, 1891.

PULISHED BY MESSRS. TWISS & SONS, ILFRACOMBE.

www.ingramcontent.com/pod-product-compliance
Lightning Source LLC
Chambersburg PA
CBHW030900050726
47500CB00009B/552